Once, in a faraway land, there was a boy who lived in the streets, a girl who lived in a palace, and a genie who lived in a lamp.

The boy was Aladdin. Aladdin was a handsome young thief who took only what he needed to survive. Often, Aladdin gave away the food he took to people even hungrier than he was. But he knew that one day, life would be better. "Just you wait, Abu," he told his pet monkey.

Aladdin had no way of knowing that far in the desert, a magical cave full of treasures was waiting just for him.

Meanwhile, in the Sultan's palace, time was running out for Princess Jasmine.

"It's the law," Jasmine's father, the Sultan, insisted. "You must marry a prince by your next birthday. And it will be your birthday in three days."

But Jasmine did not love the prince her father had chosen for her. So she ran away from home.

The world outside the palace walls was strange and scary. Jasmine did not even know that ordinary people had to pay for things. She found out, though, when she took an apple from a fruit stand and gave it to a hungry child.

Aladdin appeared in time to rescue Jasmine from the angry fruit merchant. "Forgive my poor sister. She didn't mean to steal. She's a little crazy in the head," Aladdin explained.

Later, Jasmine told her new friend why she had run away. "That's awful!" Aladdin agreed when he heard about the forced marriage.

Meanwhile, the Sultan had fallen under the spell of his evil advisor, Jafar, who wanted the Sultan's Mystique Blue Diamond.

Jafar wanted a magic lamp from the Cave of
Wonders. He needed the Sultan's diamond to
find out the name of the one person who
could enter the cave. The answer was . . .
Aladdin. Jafar immediately ordered the palace
guards to capture him.

When Aladdin was caught, he was thrown into
a dungeon. At first he could think only about
Jasmine. The guards had called her a princess.
"A princess! I can't believe it!" he said to Abu.

Then Jafar arrived, disguised as an old prisoner.
He offered to help Aladdin escape, and to find
great riches. "I need a pair of young, strong
legs like yours to go into the cave and help me
get a worthless lamp," Jafar said. "The rest of
the treasure can be yours."

Aladdin agreed.

That night, in the desert, a huge tiger's head rose up before Aladdin's astonished eyes. "Who disturbs my slumber?" the voice of the cave thundered.

"It is I! Aladdin!"

"Proceed, Aladdin!" the voice replied.

"Find the lamp first!" Jafar said as Aladdin entered the cave.

Aladdin and Abu followed a golden staircase
down, down to a chamber filled with treasures.
There was a magic carpet, too. Abu was afraid
of it, but it showed them the way to a second
chamber, where the lamp was hidden.

Then Abu, who could never resist shiny things,
grabbed a ruby. The cave trembled. "Abu has
touched the forbidden treasure. Now you will
never again see the light of day!" the
huge voice roared.

The cave began to fill with
molten lava. Aladdin pulled
Abu to safety on the Magic
Carpet just in time.

The Magic Carpet sped them to the mouth of the cave, where Jafar waited. "Help us!" Aladdin called, clinging to the rocks.

"Throw me the lamp!" cried Jafar. He snatched it from Aladdin's hand, then pulled out a dagger aiming to strike Aladdin. "What are you doing?" cried Aladdin.

In a flash, Abu had sunk his teeth into Jafar's arm saving Aladdin from the dagger. But Aladdin and Abu fell back into the cave.

Finally, the cave stopped shaking and became as silent as a tomb. "We're trapped in here," Aladdin despaired.

Abu chirped and held up his paw revealing the lamp. "Why, you hairy little thief!" Aladdin laughed when he realized the little monkey had grabbed the lamp from Jafar.

When Aladdin tried to rub some of the dust off, the lamp began to glow, and a towering cloud of smoke poured out.

"Say, you're a lot smaller than my last master," the giant shape said.

"Are you the genie of the lamp?" Aladdin asked.

"The one and only!" the Genie replied.

To prove his powers, the Genie got them out
of the cave. "I guess you're a genie all right!"
Aladdin said. "Do I get three wishes?"

"Of course!" the Genie said.

Aladdin thought of Princess Jasmine. "I wish
to be a prince!" he declared.

The next instant, the people of the city were
surprised to see an unknown handsome prince,
dressed in shining silks, riding atop an
elephant towards the palace.

"Prince Ali Ababwa," the palace guard
announced as Aladdin flew in on his magic
carpet.

"Your Majesty, I have journeyed from afar to seek your daughter's hand in marriage," Aladdin said to the astonished Sultan.

That night, Aladdin took Jasmine for a ride on the Magic Carpet. That's when she discovered he was the same kind young man she had met in the marketplace. Before the ride was over, she knew he was the one she wanted to marry.

Far below, Jafar plotted against Aladdin. He had already decided to marry the princess himself. "I must get rid of that intruder before he spoils my plans," he vowed.

So later that night, Aladdin found himself bound and gagged. Then he was thrown from a cliff into the sea.

Aladdin struggled to free one hand, and
rubbed the lamp.

"I guess you wish I'd get you out of this mess,"
the Genie said.

In the palace, Jasmine told her father she
wanted to marry Prince Ali.

But Jafar had cast another spell on the Sultan.

"You will wed Jafar," the Sultan droned.
Fortunately, Aladdin arrived and broke the spell.

Jafar fled, but not before glimpsing the lamp
hidden in Aladdin's robe. That night, he sent
his parrot, Iago, to steal the lamp from
Aladdin's room.

"I am now your master!" Jafar
bellowed when the Genie appeared.

The Genie was not too pleased with this new development. Still, he had to obey. "I wish to be sultan," Jafar commanded.

Soon, however, being sultan was not enough. "I want to be the most powerful sorcerer in the world!" Jafar said.

"I don't like it, but you got it, Master!" the Genie replied.

As his first trick, the new sorcerer banished Aladdin to the ends of the world.

Aladdin found himself trapped in a land of ice and snow. "How will I ever get out of here?" he groaned. Then he and Abu found the Magic Carpet and flew away toward the palace.

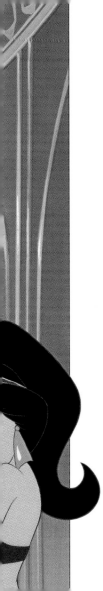

Jafar, meanwhile, had taken over the Sultan's palace and was forcing Jasmine to wait on him, and cater to all his needs.

Then Aladdin and Abu swooped into the castle. "You!" Jafar snarled. "How many times do I have to get rid of you, boy?"

The sorcerer engulfed the room in flames.

"Are you afraid to fight me, you cowardly snake?" yelled Aladdin.

"A snake, am I?" said Jafar. "So be it!" Instantly, Jafar turned himself into a huge cobra.

"Did you think you could outwit the most powerful sorcerer on earth?" the cobra hissed, preparing to strike.

Aladdin thought quickly. "The Genie has more power than you'll ever have, Jafar," he said.

"You're right!" Jafar said. He seized the lamp, and rubbed it. "Genie, my third wish is to be . . . a genie!" The cobra vanished, replaced by a huge genie shouting, "Now I have absolute power!"

Only then did Jafar notice what was happening. He was disappearing into the lamp Aladdin was holding.

And so while the evil Jafar was imprisoned in his lamp, Aladdin used his third and final wish to free his friend the Genie forever. "I'm going to miss you," Aladdin said, as the Genie prepared for his new life.

The first thing the Sultan did when he became sultan again was to change the law. Princess Jasmine could marry anyone she wished. And that's what she did. She chose Aladdin.